£1 29 ③ FEB

GW01005820

Mundarda

Mundarda, the Aboriginal name for the
Western pygmy possum, was used in 1845 by
the famous naturalist John Gould in his
book *The Mammals of Australia*.

First published in 1988 by
University of Western Australia Press
Nedlands, Western Australia 6009
under the Cygnet Books imprint.
This revised edition first published in 1993

This book is copyright. Apart from any fair dealing for the purpose of private study, research, criticism or review, as permitted under the Copyright Act 1968, no part may be reproduced by any process without written permission. Enquiries should be made to the publisher.

© Belinda Brooker 1988

National Library of Australia
Cataloguing-in-Publication entry:

Brooker, Belinda, 1967–
    Mundarda

    New ed.
    ISBN 1 875560 18 1.

    1. Burramyidae – Juvenile fiction. I. Title.

A823.3

Consultant Editor H. K. Bradbury
Design of revised edition by Susan Eve Ellvey of Designpoint, Perth
Typeset in 17pt Goudy by Lasertype, Perth
Printed through Global-Com Pte Ltd, Singapore

Mundarda

by Belinda Brooker

CYGNET BOOKS

When the moon is shining among the stars and you are snuggled up in bed, ready to go to sleep, Mundarda the pygmy possum wakes up and creeps out into the night. Mundarda is as tiny as a mouse. In fact, if you were to hold her, she would just fit neatly into your curled up hand.

As Mundarda scurries quickly among the low heath of the Western Australian bushland, she uses her big round eyes and long whiskers to find her way. She sits very still and turns her large ears towards the slightest sound, for there are many dangers in the night. An owl screeches from a far wandoo tree and the wind whispers through the dry banksia leaves . . .

It was on such a night last spring that Mundarda went in search of food and adventure. Many different kinds of flowers grew in Dryandra Forest but it was easy to find the big red eucalyptus blossoms which she loved. Mundarda poked her head right inside each flower to lick the sweet sugary nectar and soon became very full and very sticky indeed. Yellow specks of pollen stuck to her nose and whiskers and it wasn't long before she had to stop eating and clean herself.

Suddenly, Mundarda became aware of a quiet rustling in the branches below her. She sat very still, peeping over the branch, trying to discover whether the noise meant friend or foe.

Mundarda was very relieved when out of the darkness appeared a familiar little pink nose. Patch was an old friend from Dryandra Forest where Mundarda had been born. He was slightly larger than Mundarda, his fur glistened in the moonlight and there was no mistaking the large patch missing from his right ear — the result of a lucky escape from a boobook owl. Patch and Mundarda said 'hello' by touching noses and all night long they explored the bush until the soft grey light of dawn reminded them that it was time to sleep.

At sunrise, while the pygmy possums lay curled up in a dark corner, the bush began to come alive. Lizards and snakes ventured from their holes into the sun. A kangaroo started to feed on the young grass near the creek and the nest of the yellow-rumped thornbills was a hive of activity as the birds flew to and fro with food for their hungry chicks.

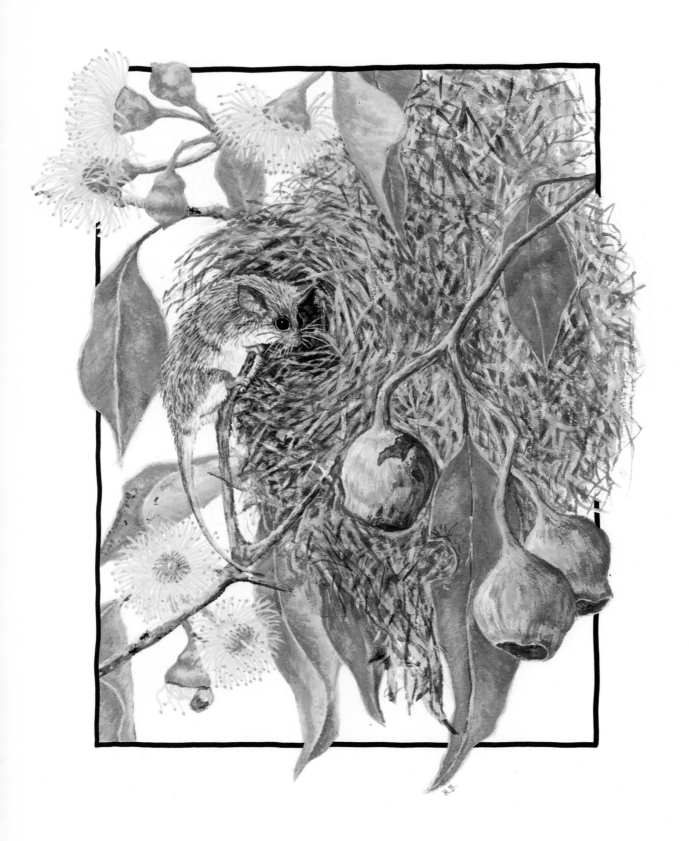

Many weeks after the thornbills had left the nest, Mundarda was exploring the bush for a soft warm hideaway for her own babies. The old thornbill's nest in the low overhanging branches of the marri tree was the perfect place. Mundarda peered inside. It was just right for the six little pygmy possum babies that were growing too large for her pouch.

As the days passed the babies grew to like their new home. They snuggled down amongst the feathers and soft grasses in the nest, huddling together for warmth and waiting for Mundarda to return and feed them. Each day the babies grew stronger and larger. Their eyes began to open and they started to move around the nest.

Soon the baby possums were big enough to go out into the bush with Mundarda. One by one they climbed out of the nest and timidly followed Mundarda along the branches. The little possums were all very curious and stopped to sniff every flower and insect. Mundarda showed them which blossoms were the best to eat.

Suddenly Mundarda saw a big feral cat in the undergrowth below. Two of the babies had sensed the danger and were hiding among the dryandra flowers. But the other baby possums were still scampering along the branches. Mundarda didn't know what to do!

Then she saw Patch and Patch saw the cat! He leapt from branch to branch with the hungry cat pouncing after him. As soon as they were out of sight Mundarda led her family to safety.

A few minutes later Patch returned looking very pleased with himself. He had escaped by hiding in the middle of a prickly hakea bush. Cats don't like prickles in their noses!

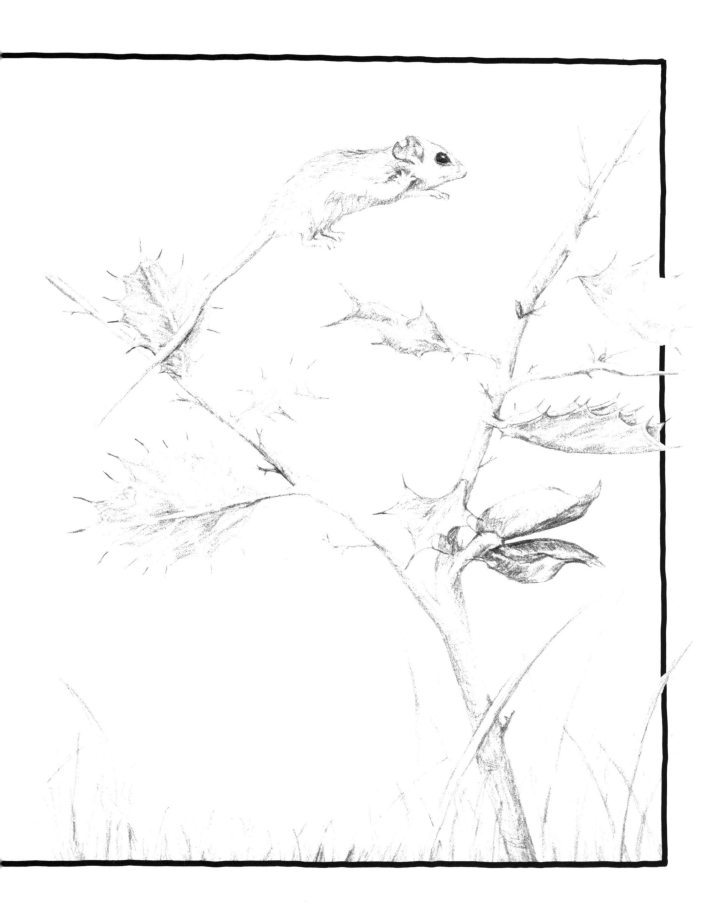

Wearily the young possums returned to the shelter of their nest. Their first night in the bush had been filled with excitement but now it was time to rest.

As the early morning sun filtered through the trees Mundarda and her family were already asleep. A new day had begun for the creatures of Dryandra Forest.

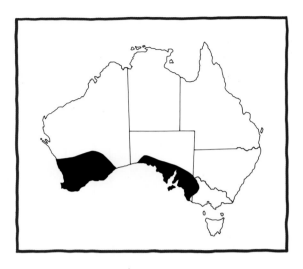

Western pygmy possum or mundarda
Cercartetus concinnus

The mundarda is a tiny Australian marsupial that weighs about 13 grams. It has soft reddish-brown fur on its back and white fur on its belly. The long gripping tail of the mundarda helps it travel through the branches of shrubs and low trees when searching for insects and nectar. Sometimes it moves across the ground but, as it only comes out at night and is very small, it is rarely seen by humans.

The female mundarda can have as many as six young at a time and up to three families, or litters, in a year. Young pygmy possums feed from six teats inside the female's pouch. They stay in the pouch for about 25 days before they are left in a nest made of leaves, grass and shredded bark.

The mundarda lives in the south-west of Western Australia and southern areas of South Australia (see map). Although this is a large area, much of the habitat of the mundarda has been destroyed by the clearing of land for farming or housing. Many still live in the national parks and scrubby woodland of Western Australia.

BELINDA BROOKER was born in New South Wales and now lives in Perth, Western Australia. She studied art at high school and zoology at The University of Western Australia. Fascinated by the animals and plants around her, Belinda has spent many hours in the Gooseberry Hill National Park assisting her father in a study of the park's birdlife. Her first book *Blue Wren* was a result of this research.

Belinda was inspired to write *Mundarda* by the pygmy possums in the nocturnal house at the Perth Zoo, and her illustrations are based on photographs and close observation of the tiny creatures.